Anna, Banana,

and the
Sleepover
Secret

Anna, Banana,

and the
Sleepover Secret

Anica Mrose Rissi

ILLUSTRATED BY Cassey Kuo

SIMON & SCHUSTER
BOOKS FOR YOUNG READERS
New York London Toronto Sydney New Delhi

SIMON & SCHUSTER BOOKS FOR YOUNG READERS
An imprint of Simon & Schuster Children's Publishing Division
1230 Avenue of the Americas, New York, New York 10020
This book is a work of fiction. Any references to historical events, real people, or real places are used fictitiously. Other names, characters, places, and events are products of the author's imagination, and any resemblance to actual events or places or persons, living or dead, is entirely coincidental.
Text copyright © 2018 by Anica Mrose Rissi
Illustrations copyright © 2018 by Cassey Kuo
All rights reserved, including the right of reproduction in whole or in part in any form.
SIMON & SCHUSTER BOOKS FOR YOUNG READERS
is a trademark of Simon & Schuster, Inc.
For information about special discounts for bulk purchases, please contact Simon & Schuster Special Sales at 1-866-506-1949 or business@simonandschuster.com.
The Simon & Schuster Speakers Bureau can bring authors to your live event. For more information or to book an event, contact the Simon & Schuster Speakers Bureau at 1-866-248-3049 or visit our website at www.simonspeakers.com.
Book design by Laurent Linn
The text for this book was set in Minister Std.
The illustrations for this book were rendered digitally.
Manufactured in the United States of America
0818 OFF
First Edition
2 4 6 8 10 9 7 5 3 1
Library of Congress Cataloging-in-Publication Data
Names: Rissi, Anica Mrose, author. | Kuo, Cassey, illustrator.
Title: Anna, Banana, and the sleepover secret / Anica Mrose Rissi ; illustrated by Cassey Kuo.
Description: First edition. | New York : Simon & Schuster Books for Young Readers, [2018] | Series: Anna, Banana ; 7 | Summary: "Anna and Sadie are excited to sleepover at Isabel's for the first time, but when a game of Truth or Dare goes wrong, they're left with a horrible secret"—Provided by publisher.
Identifiers: LCCN 2018002637 (print) | ISBN 9781534417205 (eBook) | ISBN 9781534417199 (hardback)| ISBN 9781534417182 (paperback)
Subjects: | CYAC: Sleepovers—Fiction. | Truth or dare (Game—Fiction. | Secrets—Fiction. | Best friends—Fiction. | Friendship—Fiction. | Behavior—Fiction. | BISAC: JUVENILE FICTION / Social Issues / Friendship. | JUVENILE FICTION / Animals / Dogs. | JUVENILE FICTION / Humorous Stories.
Classification: LCC PZ7.R5265 (ebook) | LCC PZ7.R5265 Any 2018 (print) | DDC [Fic]—dc23
LC record available at https://lccn.loc.gov/2018002637

For Derya
(and his parents)
—A. M. R.

To my parents and my sister, who endured my antics
and attitude since day one
—C. K.

Chapter One

Pajama Plans

"Which pajamas should I bring: the rainbow pair or the pony pair?" I asked, peering into the top drawer of my dresser.

My dog, Banana, tipped her head to one side as she considered the question.

"The rainbow ones are softer, but the pony ones are newer," I said. I grabbed both pairs and held them out for inspection. Banana sniffed each one, then nudged my left hand with her snout.

I grinned. "Rainbows it is." I returned the ponies to their drawer and tucked the rainbow pajamas into my backpack, on top of the toothbrush, hairbrush, underwear, socks, shirt, leggings, glow-in-the-dark clawed dragon-feet slippers, and sparkly nail polish that I had already packed for the sleepover. I went to my closet and stood on tiptoe to pull my sleeping bag off its high shelf, and as I turned back around with it, I heard a familiar squeak. I looked down and saw Banana holding her favorite toy, a yellow plastic bunny, in her mouth. She wagged her tail hopefully, and bit down to make it squeak again.

I bent to take it from her, and tossed it across the room. It landed in the doggy basket right next to my bed, where Banana always sleeps. She bounded over to retrieve it and carried it back to me proudly. She dropped it at my feet and looked up at me, hoping I would throw it for her again.

I knew this game: Banana wanted to distract me from packing. I hesitated, and she nosed at the toy, pushing it toward me.

I gave in. "I can't play all day," I warned her as I flicked the bunny high into the air. "Isabel's expecting us to come over soon."

Banana jumped to catch the toy before it could fall to the ground, and carried it over to my open backpack. She dropped the bunny inside. I laughed, but I also felt a twinge of guilt as I took it back out. "I'm sorry," I told her. "By 'us,' I meant Sadie and me. I can't bring you to the sleepover. Unfortunately, dogs aren't invited."

We had discussed this already. Isabel's giant

orange tabby cat, Mewsic, doesn't get along well with other animals, so it wouldn't be fair to bring Banana into Mewsic's home. I knew Banana understood that I would include her in the sleepover if I could, but that didn't stop her ears from drooping with disappointment.

I squeezed the yellow bunny, hoping its squeaks would cheer her up, and tossed it as hard as I could. Banana watched as the bunny sailed over her head and landed on the other side of the room, but she didn't even try to chase it.

"Aw, I'm going to miss you too," I said. I dropped to my knees and nuzzled my face against her soft fur. "But it's only for one night. I'll be back tomorrow morning with lots of stories to tell."

Banana's ears perked back up. She loves a good story.

"Knock knock," a voice said. Banana and I looked up to see Mom standing in the open doorway to my room. She was wearing the oversize sweatshirt my brother, Chuck, and I had given her for her last birthday. It was supersoft and had big pockets where she could put her hands if they got cold. Mom's fingers were always freezing. "You all packed for the sleepover?" she asked. I nodded. "Good. You've got just enough time for a quick lunch before Sadie's dad picks you up. Come on downstairs. Dad's making grilled cheese."

"Cheese!" I cheered, and Banana twirled in a

circle, chasing her own tail with excitement. She loves cheese almost as much as she loves stories.

Banana led the way out of my room, and I raced down the stairs after her. We both knew I would sneak her a small bite of cheese if I got the chance. I wasn't really supposed to feed her at the table, of course, but Mom and Dad didn't have to know.

It would be our little secret.

Chapter Two

Cheese, Please

The grilled cheese sandwiches were delicious. Dad made mine with sliced pickles and mustard, just how I like it, and there was so much cheese, some oozed out the edges. He didn't even notice when I dropped a bite of cheddar for Banana. She caught it before it reached the floor, then sat at my feet in case I might drop more. Banana is always hopeful, especially about cheese.

When I'd finished the last bite, I let her lick the extra cheesiness off my fingertips. I squirmed a little as her tongue and whiskers tickled my skin. "Don't forget that Banana gets two scoops of kibble tonight for dinner," I told my brother. "And she'll need walks in the afternoon *and* before bed."

"Right," Chuck said, rolling his eyes. "Two walks for dinner and a scoop of kibble in bed. Got it."

Banana wagged her tail at the joke, but I didn't think it was funny. I wanted Chuck to take this seriously. "This is Banana's first night without me," I reminded him. "You have to *promise* to take good care of her."

I had been to Isabel's house plenty of times, but this would be my first sleepover there. Usually the sleepovers we had were at my house, and when we spent the night at Sadie's dad's house, Banana was invited too. Banana couldn't go to Sadie's mom's place—she had a strict No Pets rule—but we hadn't had a sleepover there in a while. Not since before I got Banana. Banana had slept in her basket next to my bed, with me *in* the bed, almost every night of her life. I hoped she wouldn't be too lonely tonight.

"Don't worry, Anna. We'll take good care of her," Dad said. "I'm sure Banana will miss you, but we'll keep her busy and happy while you're gone."

"Yeah. And I'll try to fart a lot so it will smell like you're still here," Chuck teased.

"*Charles,*" Mom said in her *That's enough* voice. Before I could think of a good comeback, we heard a car horn honk in the driveway.

"Sadie's here!" I cried. I slid off my chair, carried my dirty dishes to the sink, and ran upstairs to grab my backpack, sleeping bag, and pillow.

When I came back down, Sadie was standing inside with a big grin on her face. I smiled back. "Hey!" I said.

"Hi! Are you ready? It's sleepover time!" Sadie did a silly little dance that made Banana bark and jump at her feet. I danced around too, as best I could while holding all my sleepover stuff. Soon we were laughing so hard, I had to stop so I wouldn't fall over. Sadie held out her arms to take my sleeping bag and pillow so I could hug

my parents and Banana good-bye.

"Have fun, kiddo," Dad said.

"And be good," Mom added.

"I will," I answered them both. I bent down

to pet Banana's soft ears and kissed her on the forehead. "You too, Banana: Have fun and be good." Banana looked sad, but she licked me on the nose to agree anyway, and I giggled.

I followed Sadie out the door and toward her dad's car in the driveway. "Don't say anything in front of my dad, but I brought us a secret surprise," she said.

The word "secret" lit my brain up like a sparkler. "What is it?" I asked.

Sadie zipped her lips and opened the car door without answering. The secret would have to wait.

Chapter Three
Hurry Up and Wait

I hoped Sadie would at least give me a hint about the secret on the car ride, but instead, she talked her dad into turning the radio up full blast, and we sang along to the music. One of 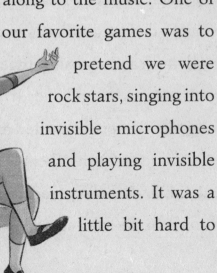 our favorite games was to pretend we were rock stars, singing into invisible microphones and playing invisible instruments. It was a little bit hard to play imaginary drums with my seat belt strapped on tight, but I still crashed down on the cymbals and twirled my drumstick while Sadie played air guitar. We belted the chorus with her dad singing backup, and by the time we reached Isabel's street, I was pumped with so much energy, I almost forgot about Sadie's surprise.

Isabel ran out to greet us as the car pulled into her driveway, and Sadie and I unbuckled and scrambled out the second we came to a stop. Sadie's dad laughed at how we were jumping up and down and squealing together in the driveway, but none of us minded. It was sleepover time! My friends were as excited as I was.

"Good luck with them!" Sadie's dad called to Abuelita, Isabel's grandmother, who waved to him from the front steps and welcomed us inside.

"Let's go up to my room!" Isabel said after we'd said hello to Abuelita and Isabel's parents. We followed Isabel up the stairs to the bedroom she shares with her sister Luisa. Isabel and Luisa's room is across the hall from the bedroom their two oldest sisters, Emma and Maria, share.

Isabel and Luisa's room is usually messy on Isabel's side and neat on Luisa's side, but today it was neat everywhere. I guessed Isabel's parents had made her clean up before Sadie and I came over.

"Luisa's sleeping in Emma and Maria's room tonight, so we get the whole place to ourselves," Isabel said. She plopped down on her bed, and Mewsic, the cat, jumped off it, disappearing underneath.

Unlike Banana, who wants to greet every visitor the second they walk in the door, Mewsic always takes a while to warm up to people—even people he already knows, like Sadie and me. We weren't offended, though. We knew he would come out when he was ready.

We put our backpacks, pillows, and sleeping bags down on the floor next to Isabel's bed. "Oooh, did you get new nail polish colors?" Sadie asked, looking at the collection of bottles on Isabel's dresser.

Isabel shook her head. "Maria let me borrow hers for when we do pedicures later. And I got out all the board games and puzzles for us too." Isabel waved her hand toward a stack of games on her desk. "What should we do first?"

Pedicures and games sounded fun, but what

I really wanted was to hear about Sadie's secret. "Is it time for the surprise yet?" I said.

Isabel looked back and forth between us. "What surprise?" she asked. Sadie grinned.

Excitement zipped through me like two squirrels playing chase around a tree. I thought of the word of the day our teacher, Ms. Burland, had written on the board last Wednesday: "anticipate." *Anticipate: to look forward to or expect,* it had said. It was fun having a surprise to anticipate, and it was twice as fun anticipating it together. Now I was glad Sadie hadn't told me the secret on the car ride, so I could find out about it at the same time Isabel did.

Sadie opened her backpack, reached deep inside, and took something out. We couldn't see what it was yet because she kept it hidden in her palms. Finally, she lifted one hand with a flourish to reveal the secret thing she held. "Ta-da!" she exclaimed.

Chapter Four

The Secret Surprise

Isabel burst out laughing. "Is that . . . a lemon?" she asked, pointing at the object in Sadie's outstretched hand.

"Yup!" Sadie said. "Surprise!"

I laughed too. I was definitely surprised, but also confused. "Um, Sadie? Why did you bring a *lemon* to the sleepover?" I asked.

Sadie joined the giggling. "That's the surprise part!" she said. She wiggled her eyebrows dramatically. Even though she had just shown us the surprise, she was still being secretive about it. "It *does* something secret."

I leaned closer to look. It seemed like a normal lemon, not a plastic one or something else in disguise. "Is it for making lemonade? Or baking lemon bars?" I asked.

"Or squirting at enemies and intruders?" Isabel guessed. We laughed harder.

"Nope! It's for writing secret messages," Sadie explained. Except, that didn't actually

explain anything. I was still confused.

Isabel scrunched her eyebrows together and tipped her head to one side, like Banana had done earlier. She clearly didn't know what Sadie was talking about any more than I did. "You want us to write secret messages on a lemon?" she said.

"No, silly. We'll write the messages on paper. We're going to use the lemon juice as invisible ink. Whatever we write with it will dry to be invisible. No one will even know that the secret messages are there," Sadie said.

That sounded neat, but . . . "But how will *we* see the messages?" I asked.

Sadie had an answer for that, too. "You hold the paper up to a source of heat, like a lightbulb or a hair dryer, and the heat makes the ink appear," she told us.

"Cool! I never knew lemons were magic," I said.

Isabel poked the lemon and pulled her finger back quickly, like she expected the fruit to bite. "Have you tried it?" she asked.

Sadie shook her head. "Nope. I just read about it in a book of science experiments. I was waiting to try it with you guys."

"Let's do it!" Isabel said. We followed her down to the kitchen, where Isabel's mom agreed to slice the lemon in half for us, even though Isabel wouldn't tell her what we planned to do with it. "Nothing bad or messy, I promise," Isabel said. "Just top secret."

"Well then, I'll leave you to it," her mom said with a smile. She waved away our chorus of thank-yous and left the room.

Isabel got out a bowl, and we took turns

squeezing the lemon halves over it until all the juice was out. I fished the seeds out of the juice with a spoon while Sadie grabbed a dish towel to clean up the drops that had squirted onto the counter and Isabel ran to get paper for us to write on and cotton swabs for dipping into the "ink."

"You should carry the bowl up the stairs, Anna," Isabel said when she'd returned with the supplies. "You're the steadiest one of us. Remember the balancing game?" Sadie nodded in agreement. Last month we'd done a challenge at recess to see who in our class could stand on one foot the longest, and I'd outlasted everyone except Timothy and Keisha. I felt proud that my friends remembered that.

I held the bowl in both hands and walked carefully so I wouldn't spill as we went back upstairs and into Isabel's bedroom. Isabel put the paper and cotton swabs on the floor, and I set the bowl down next to them. We all sat crisscross applesauce around the supplies. "What kind of secret message should we write?" I asked.

"Maybe we should each write a secret wish," Isabel said. "I bet the magic lemon juice will help the wishes come true."

"Yeah!" I said.

Sadie grinned. "It's *science*, not magic. But secret wishes are a great idea."

I dipped my cotton swab into the lemon juice and looked at the blank page on the floor in front of me, wondering what I should fill it with. I glanced at my friends. Sadie moved her cotton swab slowly over her page, writing neatly. Isabel bent over her page and worked quickly, making wet lines that soaked into the paper and disappeared. It looked like she was drawing her wish, not writing it, which was no surprise. Isabel loves to draw and is really good at it. She's probably the best artist in our class.

I couldn't choose whether to write or draw, so I decided I would do both. But what should my secret wish be?

I saw something move out of the corner of my eye and looked to see Mewsic poking his nose out from under the bed. He wanted in on the secrets too! "Hey, kitty kitty," I said, but softly, so as not to scare him. He inched a little closer and his whiskers twitched. I wished he weren't so shy so I could pet him.

That gave me an idea. I put the cotton swab against the page and started drawing my favorite thing: Banana. Using invisible ink was harder than I'd expected because the lines I drew kept disappearing, but it was fun to try. I grinned at my friends. I couldn't wait to find out what secret things they were putting on their papers.

I dipped the cotton swab back into the ink. Next to where I'd drawn Banana, I drew Mewsic, nose-to-nose with her. Across the top I wrote *Banana meets Mewsic!* I added speech balloons above their heads, with Banana saying *Hi!* and Mewsic saying *Purrrrr.*

That was my secret wish: that Banana and Mewsic could meet and get along, so we could all be at sleepovers at Isabel's house together. I knew it wouldn't happen—the lemon juice would have to be *really* magic to cause that—but drawing it made me feel a little like Banana was here with me. I couldn't wait to see how the wish would look once the ink became visible.

Isabel's second-oldest sister, Emma, skipped into the room. The skipping startled Mewsic, who darted back under the bed. "What are you guys doing?" Emma asked. She stood over us and stared down at our papers. I started to cover mine to keep it private, then laughed as I realized it didn't matter—the ink was invisible! She could look right at it and not see my masterpiece. *I* couldn't even see it.

"Drawing," Isabel answered, at the same time Sadie said, "Writing secrets!"

Emma's face twisted up with confusion. "I don't see anything," she said.

My friends and I grinned at one another. "Exactly!" Isabel said.

"Mission accomplished," I added.

Emma rolled her eyes. "Okay then. Have fun with your invisible art." She turned back around and flounced out of the room. Mewsic ran out the door behind her.

"I think mine's done," Sadie said. "Now it just has to dry."

"Mine too," I said.

"Mine three!" Isabel said. "What should we do while we wait?"

"Is it too early for Truth or Dare?" I asked.

Sadie made a supervillain face. "It's never too early for Truth or Dare."

Chapter Five
If You Dare

Isabel stood up. "Let's play in the living room. We can leave our secret wishes here, since no one can see them anyway."

We went downstairs and found Mewsic curled up on one end of the big red couch. I expected him to run away, but instead, he flicked his tail and blinked at us, then went on with his nap. I guessed he was getting used to us being around. I was glad.

Isabel sat on the couch beside him, and Sadie and I plopped down next to her. Isabel tucked her feet up under her body as she turned to face Sadie. "Truth or dare?" she asked.

"Dare," Sadie said immediately, and Isabel and I grinned. Sadie always chooses dare.

"I dare you . . ." Isabel said the words slowly while she thought about what dare to give. Her eyes sparkled with inspiration. "I dare you to go up to Maria and ask if the refrigerator is still running. And when she says yes, you say, 'Then you'd better catch it!'"

I giggled and Sadie groaned. "That's so corny!" she said, falling back against the couch cushions. "You couldn't give me something less embarrassing?"

"That's what makes it a good dare!" Isabel said. She looked as gleeful as Banana does when she finds a forgotten tennis ball. Mewsic stretched a paw across Isabel's lap and leaned his weight against her leg. He looked pretty pleased too.

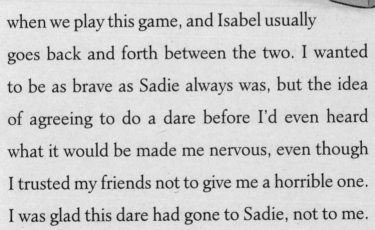

Sadie jumped to her feet. She never turns down a dare. I almost always choose truth when we play this game, and Isabel usually goes back and forth between the two. I wanted to be as brave as Sadie always was, but the idea of agreeing to do a dare before I'd even heard what it would be made me nervous, even though I trusted my friends not to give me a horrible one. I was glad this dare had gone to Sadie, not to me.

Sadie smoothed her skirt and looked up the stairs. "Is Maria in her room?"

"I think so," Isabel said. We stood up too. Mewsic narrowed his eyes, like he was annoyed that Isabel was no longer being his pillow. He curled himself around one of the real couch pillows instead.

Sadie crept up the stairs like she was a spy on a secret mission. She hunched her shoulders to make herself smaller and moved with slow, light steps, like Banana does when she's trying to sneak up on a squirrel. Isabel and I followed behind her, covering our mouths with our hands to keep the giggles inside. Already this was the most fun game of Truth or Dare ever.

Sadie paused at the top of the stairs. She turned and put her fingers to her lips as if to say *Shhhhhh!* and motioned for us to hide. Isabel and I flattened ourselves against the wall to stay out of sight as Sadie raised her fist and knocked twice on Emma and Maria's bedroom door.

"Come in!" Maria called, and Isabel let out a tiny snort that made me want to laugh out loud too. I tried not to look at her, but I could feel her shaking with silent giggles beside me.

Sadie kept her cool, though. She turned the doorknob, pushed open the door, and stepped inside their room.

"I was just wondering . . . do you think the refrigerator is still running?" we heard her say. Isabel bit her fist and nudged me with her shoulder. I nudged back. Sadie was so bold.

"Huh? Why wouldn't it be?" Maria said. "Wait, is this some kind of—"

"Oh no!" Sadie shouted, playing her part to the fullest. "We have to catch it! Run!" She bolted out of the bedroom, shrieking at a high pitch. Isabel grabbed my hand, and we ran down the stairs after her, gasping with laughter and scaring Mewsic, who leaped off the couch and quickly disappeared.

All three of us collapsed on the couch on top of one another.

A voice cut through our giggles. "What's going on in there?"

Chapter Six

Party Crashers

I looked up and saw Isabel's mother standing in the doorway, her hands on her hips. "Nothing!" Isabel gasped out as she tried to catch her breath from laughing. "Just having fun."

"Hmmm," her mother said. "Maybe the fun could be had a little more softly."

Sadie, Isabel, and I scrambled to sit up and look innocent. "Sorry.

We'll keep it down," Isabel said. Her mom smiled and left the room.

"I hope we didn't get you in trouble," Sadie said, echoing my thoughts.

"No, it's okay. She's not mad at us," Isabel said.

"Good," Sadie said. I nodded in agreement. I hate making parents upset—mine or anyone else's.

"We'll just have to dare each other a little more quietly," Isabel said. "But, oh my gosh, I can't believe how well you pulled that off."

"Yeah," I said. "That was epic." "Epic" was a word I had learned from Chuck. He used it to mean "super impressive" or "huge." Sadie's face filled with pride.

Maria came into the living room with Emma and Luisa close behind her. "What was *that* all about?" she asked.

Sadie shrugged and smiled sheepishly. "Sorry. It was a dare. I had to do it."

"Oooh, are you playing Truth or Dare?" Luisa asked, stepping toward us. We nodded. "I want to play!" She squeezed into the space on the couch between Isabel and me. I moved over, practically onto the armrest, to make room.

Maria dropped cross-legged onto the floor, and Emma settled beside her. "We'll all play," Maria announced. Isabel, Sadie, and I looked at one another in surprise. Sometimes Luisa hung out with us if she didn't have anything better to

do, but Emma and Maria almost never did. It was kind of exciting that they wanted to join our game. Isabel's older sisters were all pretty cool. "Whose turn is it?" Maria asked.

"Uh, Sadie's the only one who's gone so far," Isabel said. "So I guess it's—"

"I'll ask," Emma interrupted. "Isabel, truth or dare?"

I glanced at Isabel. Usually the person who'd just done a dare or truth got to ask next, but Emma was way older than us—she was already in seventh grade, and Maria was in eighth—so even Sadie didn't correct her. Apparently, we were playing by their rules now.

"Truth," Isabel said.

Emma leaned forward. "Okay, truth: Who do you like better, Anna or Sadie?"

Chapter Seven
The Terrible Truth

My whole body froze when I heard Emma's question, except I could feel how quickly my heart was still beating. I both did and didn't want to hear Isabel's answer. Who would she choose?

But Isabel just rolled her eyes. "Both!" she said. I let out my breath. Of course that was true.

Emma shook her head. "Sure, but if you *had* to choose between them, who would you choose?"

Now I knew for sure that Emma was trying to stir up trouble. I glanced at Sadie. She looked as uneasy as I felt. But Isabel didn't hesitate at all.

"I would choose Sadie for making up rules to new games and taking charge and laughing loudest and being super brave about doing silly dares. And I would choose Anna for sharing books with and knowing cool words and inventing recipes and having the best dog ever," she said.

I felt a smile growing inside me, and saw one spread across Sadie's face. "But my *favorite* is being best friends with both of them and all three of us hanging out together," Isabel finished. She winked at me, and I winked back. I felt the same way, and I knew Sadie did too.

Emma leaned back onto her elbows and sighed. I could see she was giving up. "Fine," she said.

Isabel grinned. "My turn to ask," she said, returning the game to its original rules. Sadie nodded her approval.

Isabel turned to her oldest sister. "Maria. Truth or dare?"

"Hmmm. Truth," Maria said.

"Okay, tell the truth: Did you really stay late after school for extra cello practice last Wednesday?" Isabel's voice was barely louder than a whisper. I guessed she wanted to make sure no parents overheard.

Maria blushed dark red. Emma giggled, and Luisa's eyes grew wide. "No," Maria said. "I wanted to watch the girls' basketball tryouts to cheer on my friends, but I didn't think Mom would say yes to my sticking around for that."

"I knew it!" Isabel cried. She pumped her fist into the air.

"But I *did* practice extra on my own that day, before tryouts started," Maria added. "And Tawana and Kaye both made the team, so it was worth it."

"Liar, liar, pants on fire," Emma teased, and Maria stuck out her tongue in response. I wondered what would have happened if she'd told her parents the truth. It seemed like a weird thing to lie about.

"Your turn to ask someone," Sadie said to Maria, sounding a little impatient. I could tell she didn't love how Isabel's sisters were taking over our game. I didn't like it either, but it felt like we had no choice but to let them. After all, we were playing in *their* living room. But I hoped that after this we'd go back to doing something with just the three of us.

"Okay, let's see . . ." Maria moved her finger through the air, pointing it at each of us, as she decided who to choose. The finger stopped on me, and my heart skipped a beat. "Anna," she said. "Truth or dare?"

Chapter Eight

Someone Else's Secret

I swallowed hard. Why was I so nervous? Maybe because of the way Maria was looking at me, like she was a cat and I was a mouse, and she thought I might taste delicious. I tried to puff myself up bigger as I prepared for her to pounce. "Truth," I said. No way would I risk a dare with Maria as the one choosing it.

Maria licked her lips. "All right, truth," she said. "How about . . . what's something you know about Sadie that she wouldn't want you to tell us?"

My jaw fell open. That was the meanest Truth or Dare question I'd ever heard in my life. Isabel, Sadie, and Luisa looked shocked by it too.

"No," I said, without even worrying about what Maria might think. "I'm not doing that."

"You have to!" Emma said. "You chose truth!" Maria nodded.

I shook my head, feeling much braver on Sadie's behalf than I ever would have been on my own. I knew lots of Sadie's secrets—small ones, big ones, good ones, embarrassing ones—and Isabel did too. But they were called "secrets" for a reason, and Sadie was one of my two best friends. No way was I going to spill her secrets and break her trust. This "truth" was completely unfair. "I won't answer that. You can ask anything you want about *me,* but I won't share secrets that belong to someone else," I said. My voice was as firm as Mom's when she tells Banana "No chewing!" if Banana sniffs Mom's shoes.

Sadie shot me a grateful look, but I knew she would have done the same thing for me.

"When you choose truth, you *have* to answer with the truth. Those are the rules," Maria said. But I could tell Isabel and Luisa were on our side. That made four against two. Maria and Emma were not going to win this, even if it meant ending the game and letting them think I was chicken.

Sadie spoke up. "Actually, she doesn't have to. There's a rule in Truth or Dare that once per game, each player can turn down a dare and take a truth instead, or turn down a truth to do a dare. So, Anna's not breaking the rules if she switches to dare now. It's her choice."

I had never heard that rule before. I was pretty sure Sadie had made it up right then to save me, but Luisa said, "Yeah," and Isabel added, "Everyone knows that," so I pretended I'd known about it all along too.

Emma looked like she wanted to keep fighting, but Maria shrugged her shoulders and said, "Okay, fine. We'll let you do a dare instead, if that's what you really want."

Normally, choosing dare made me super-duper nervous, but this time it felt like a giant relief. "Yes, please. Dare," I said, and waited to hear my fate.

Chapter Nine

The Challenge

Maria looked around the room for inspiration. She pointed to the wall behind me, which was lined with shelves holding picture frames, knickknacks, and lots and lots of books. Isabel's grandmother is a librarian, and the entire family loves to read. Their house has so many books, it would take a whole lifetime to read them all.

"See that vase?" Maria asked.

I swiveled to look and spotted it on a middle shelf. "Yeah," I said.

"I dare you to balance it on your head for ten seconds," she said.

A small rush of panic shot through me, like always happens when I'm challenged with a dare. But just as quickly as it had zinged into my chest, the panic disappeared. That wasn't such a terrible dare. I could do it.

I jumped up from the couch and took the vase off the shelf. It was lighter than I'd expected, given how big it was. It was sculpted from thin clay and hand-painted with delicate flowers up the sides. It was beautiful. I wondered who had made it.

"Wait," Luisa said. "I don't think that's a good idea."

Isabel's eyebrows were pushed close together. "Yeah, isn't that the vase Abuelita's mother gave our parents on their wedding day? I think it's really old and special," she said.

I gripped the vase a little tighter, suddenly worried I might drop it. "It's fine," Maria said. "She can stand on the carpet while she does the dare, and the carpet will cushion the fall. *If* it falls," she added. She crossed her arms and raised both eyebrows. "Or she can always go back to choosing truth if she'd rather just answer the question."

I looked to Sadie for help. Sadie bit her bottom lip like she does when she's worried, but she didn't say what she thought I should do.

Isabel was also looking at Sadie. "Well . . ." Isabel said. "Anna *does* have really good balance." She turned to me. "And you'd be super careful, right?"

I hesitated. The dare made me nervous, especially knowing how special the vase was. But Sadie's eyes were filled with so much hope, I couldn't back out now. Going back to "truth" just wasn't an option. "Right," I said with way more confidence than I felt. Sadie looked relieved.

I took a deep breath and nodded at my friends. "Okay. I'll do the dare," I said. They nodded back grimly. I walked slowly to the center of the carpet, taking my time to get there, even though I also just wanted to get this whole thing over with.

"No hands," Emma said, as if I didn't know that. I resisted the urge to glare at her.

I faced Sadie and Isabel for good luck, lifted the vase up high with both hands, and placed it on my head. I moved its base to the flattest spot on my skull that I could find, the spot just above my forehead. Then I steadied my breathing and let go.

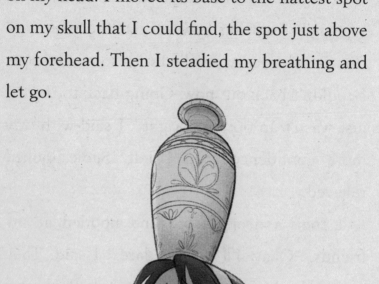

Chapter Ten

Dare, Dare, Don't!

"One! . . . Two! . . ." Luisa said, counting off the seconds. I held my arms out to my sides to help keep my balance and tried not to move my head. So far the vase was holding steady.

"Three! . . . Four! . . ." she said, and the other girls joined in, counting together in unison. It felt like they were cheering me on, even Emma and Maria.

"Five! . . . Six! . . ." they all said, and I could hear Sadie's and Isabel's voices climbing higher with excitement. I felt hope and excitement building inside me, too. Six seconds! Only four more to go! I was doing it! I was pulling off the dare!

"Seven! . . . Eight! . . ." the girls called, and for a second I thought I felt the vase almost tip, but I moved my head just slightly to steady it, and somehow it stayed in place.

My heart was pounding harder than if I'd just run full speed around the bases in kickball. Only two more seconds! I was almost, almost there.

"Nine!" they practically shouted, and out of the corner of my eye I saw a streak of orange fur as Mewsic ran out from his hiding place underneath the couch and dashed right in front of me, hurrying out of the room. I blinked with surprise and jerked my arms up to make sure the vase held steady.

"Ten!" Isabel, Sadie, Maria,

Emma, and Luisa cried, at the same time I shouted, "*No!*" and felt the vase toppling off my head.

My hands moved faster than they'd ever moved before, reaching to grab the vase as it fell. I caught it in one hand, then the other, but I was falling forward too, and it slipped through my grip as I stumbled. Isabel dove to catch it, like Banana leaping to fetch a Frisbee. She flew

through the air, and it fell through her hands right before she hit the ground.

The vase struck the carpet with a *thud* and broke in two.

Chapter Eleven

Too Many Secrets

"Oh no," Isabel said. She knelt beside the pieces.

"Oh no, oh no, oh no," her sister Luisa echoed, running to her side.

I couldn't say anything. I was frozen in place, staring at the broken vase in shock. What had I done? I was going to be in so much trouble.

I wished I could rewind those fifteen seconds, back to before I balanced the vase on my head, back to before I took on that stupid dare. Back to the moment where I could have said no.

What had I been thinking, agreeing to do a thing like that?

I looked up and met Sadie's eyes. She looked as guilty and horrified as I felt inside. What were we going to do?

"I'm sorry," I said, the words rushing out of me like Mewsic had rushed across the room. "I'm so sorry. I'm *really* sorry."

Sadie grabbed my hand and squeezed it, and I knew she wished as badly as I did that we could fix this.

Isabel shook her head. "It's my fault too. I knew the vase was fragile. I shouldn't have let you take the dare. I just didn't think *this* would happen." Hearing Isabel take the blame made me feel even worse. *She* wasn't the one who'd dared me. She looked up at her sisters, who hovered around us, looking upset. "What are we going to tell our parents?"

Maria blinked slowly. "Nothing," she said. "We'll tell them nothing."

Isabel looked startled. "What do you mean?" she asked.

Emma stepped forward. "That's right. None of you are going to say one word about this to Mom and Dad."

"But—" Luisa said, before Maria cut her off with a look.

"Do you want them to ground us forever?" she asked.

"No, but—" Isabel started to say.

"And for Anna and Sadie to never be invited over again?" Emma interrupted.

Sadie and I looked at each other in panic.

Isabel's parents wouldn't really ban us from their house forever . . . would they?

I swallowed hard. Getting Isabel grounded and Sadie and me banned for life was the last thing I wanted. But just *not* telling their parents wasn't going to fix this. As my Nana always says, two wrongs don't make a right.

"I'm the one who dropped it," I said. "I'll tell them what happened and that it was all my fault. Isabel and Sadie shouldn't get in trouble too because of me. Maybe I can save up my allowance and do extra chores until I can buy them a new vase to replace it."

Luisa looked like she might burst into tears. "That vase was, like, a hundred years old. I don't think you can get another one."

I looked down at the vase and felt like I

might break in half too. This was awful.

Maria crossed her arms. "If you tell them what happened, we'll *all* get in trouble. Even though Anna is the one who dropped it, all of us were involved."

"I wasn't," Luisa said.

"That won't matter. They'll blame us because we're older and because Maria dared her and we all said she should," Emma said.

"*I* didn't say she should," Luisa pointed out. The older girls ignored her.

"But don't we still have to explain why the vase is broken?" Isabel asked.

"Not if they don't see it," Emma said. She opened a giant cabinet, pulled out a tablecloth, and knelt on the floor next to Isabel. She frowned as she placed the two halves of the broken vase inside the cloth, wrapped them up carefully, carried the bundle back to the cabinet, and tucked the evidence deep inside.

"There," Emma said. "Now no one has to know. It's our secret."

Chapter Twelve
The Problem with Promises

Up in Isabel's room, Sadie and I sank down onto the carpet next to our backpacks while Isabel shut the door behind us. She let out a huge sigh, then sat on the floor next to us. We all leaned back against the bed.

"I really am sorry," I said, even though I knew those words wouldn't fix this.

Isabel pulled my pillow onto her lap and hugged it against her chest. "I would have done the dare too, to protect Sadie's secrets. That was a horrible choice they gave you. I'm sorry I let them take over our game."

Sadie twisted the end of her ponytail around one finger. I knew she was tempted to chew on it, like she sometimes did when she was upset, but she was trying hard to break that habit. "Do you think we should tell your parents anyway? Even though you promised your sisters we wouldn't?" she asked.

Before we'd gone upstairs, Maria had made Isabel pinky-swear that none of us would tell their mom and dad what had happened.

"I don't know," Isabel said. She rested her chin on the pillow. "Then my sisters *and* my parents will be mad at me."

"Even if we tell them it was all my fault?" I said. I didn't want anyone getting mad at me either, but I *was* the one who had broken the vase.

"It wasn't all your fault, though. You broke it, but Maria gave you the dare and Emma pressured you into it, and none of the rest of us stopped you. Any one of us saying no could have changed what happened. That's how my parents will see it, anyway," Isabel said, and I could see how that was right.

"They're going to find out eventually, though, aren't they?" Sadie said. "I mean, it's not like vases just *disappear*. When they notice it's gone, they'll know something happened to it. We can't keep this a secret forever."

Isabel looked ready to cry, which was exactly how I felt. "I don't know," she repeated. "I'm not going to lie about it. If they ask me what happened, I'll tell them the truth. But maybe Emma's right. Maybe they won't notice it's missing, at least not until we've figured out how to replace it or something." She burrowed her face in the pillow for a moment, then looked up and said, "Can we please just forget it for now? I don't want this to ruin our sleepover. Especially if it ends up being the last sleepover I'm allowed to have."

Sadie and I glanced at each other. "Okay," she said.

"Okay," I echoed, because I didn't know what else to do. I hoped that agreeing would stop Isabel from crying, but I could see the tears forming in the corners of her eyes.

Just when I thought I might start crying too, Sadie shrieked and jumped up, then plopped back down beside us and burst into hysterical laughter.

Isabel and I stared at her. My heart was racing at full gallop, but at least being startled had chased away my tears. "What happened?" I asked.

"Mewsic!" Sadie said. She pointed, and I saw what had caused her surprise: A small orange paw poked out from under the bed, then disappeared back under it. "He grabbed on to my dress like it was a toy, and I screamed because I hadn't even known he was under there. He scared me!"

I smiled with relief and felt the giggles bubble up inside of me, too. It was nice to have something to laugh about again.

"Here, silly kitty," Isabel cooed. She lifted the comforter and pulled Mewsic out for petting.

"Meow," Mewsic protested, but he didn't run away.

I touched his soft fur and felt like maybe things would turn out all right.

Chapter Thirteen
Meow Yeow

When Mewsic had had enough petting and we were all feeling a little better, we got back to the fun of the sleepover. Sadie gathered our invisible wishes and put those aside. None of us felt like dealing with more secrets or playing more Truth or Dare, so we turned on some music, took off our socks, and transformed the room into a spa. We wove paper towels between our toes to keep them separated and took turns painting one another's toenails. Isabel painted Sadie's left foot with a different color polish on each toe, and I did her right foot with pink and purple swirls.

Then Sadie and I painted Isabel's toenails bright yellow with dark blue polka dots, and Sadie and Isabel made mine pink with a layer of glitter polish on top. While our toes dried, Sadie redid Isabel's braids, and I loaned her my favorite headband to top the style off. I held still while Sadie styled my hair into a french braid, and Isabel tied Sadie's ponytail full of ribbons. By the time we got called downstairs for dinner, we were looking extra sparkly and feeling a lot better.

We got to make our own personal pizzas for dinner, and I loaded mine with tomato sauce and cheese, and used the chopped green peppers to decorate it with a smiley face. Sadie did the same with her pizza but used pepperoni for eyes, and Isabel put so many different toppings on hers that there wasn't even room for a face. It was such fun, I almost forgot about the broken vase, until Isabel's dad said something nice about our pizzas looking creative and the guilt came back, gluing itself to my insides. Even taking a big gulp of water couldn't wash it away.

I didn't say anything about it to Isabel, though. If she had managed to get distracted enough to forget about the vase like she'd wanted, I certainly wasn't going to remind her. Besides, her three sisters were eating their pizzas nearby, and Emma was watching us as closely as Banana watches Chuck when she thinks he might drop some cheese. I didn't want her to get suspicious that we might break Isabel's promise.

For the rest of the night we acted like the disaster had never happened, and so it was almost like it *hadn't*. Almost.

But I knew it had.

It didn't feel good keeping that secret inside me, even knowing my friends were carrying it too. It made my belly ache. It made my smile less real. And it made me miss Banana terribly. I couldn't bring up the secret with Isabel and Sadie, but if Banana were here, I could have talked it through with her. She would listen and understand. She might even help me figure out what to do. She definitely would comfort me with a cuddle and a lick.

I wanted that so badly, but Banana *wasn't* here. I had ruined the vase. It was ruining the sleepover. And I was stuck keeping the secret.

Chapter Fourteen

A Squeaky Surprise

By the time Isabel's dad knocked on the door and told us it was time for pajamas and toothbrushing, I was exhausted from worrying about the secret for so long. Isabel asked her father, "Can we play just one more round of Uno?" but I was already returning my playing cards to the deck.

"Nope. It's already well past your usual bedtime, and Mom and I want to get to bed ourselves soon too," he said. I groaned along with Isabel and Sadie, but secretly, I felt relieved. I couldn't wait to fall fast asleep, so that soon it would be morning and I could go home and tell Banana everything.

I unzipped my backpack to take out my dragon-feet slippers, rainbow pajamas, and toothbrush, and saw something unexpected inside. It was Banana's yellow plastic bunny toy. I pulled it out and squeezed it. My heart pinched with sadness as it squeaked.

Sadie looked over and giggled. "You brought

Banana's toy to the sleepover?" she asked.

I shook my head. "I didn't know it was in there. Banana must have dropped it inside my backpack again when I wasn't looking. It's her favorite toy. I hope she isn't missing it."

"Maybe she wanted you to have it tonight, since she couldn't be here with you," Isabel said.

I liked that idea, but I worried about Banana being lonely without me, and without her favorite toy, too. I squeezed it again, and it made me wish I could see the way Banana's ears always lift up when she hears it. I wondered what she was doing right then and if she missed me as much as I was missing her.

We changed into pajamas, brushed our teeth, and unrolled our sleeping bags. I tucked the yellow bunny inside mine with me. I hoped I wouldn't roll onto it in the middle of the night and wake everyone up with its squeak, but it seemed worth the risk. I felt a little bit better just having it there beside me. If that had been Banana's plan, it was a good one.

Isabel's mom stopped by to turn out the lights and wish us sweet dreams, and it felt so nice to have my head on the pillow, I was certain I would be asleep in no time.

But I was wrong.

Instead of winding down until I drifted off to sleep, my brain cranked up in the opposite direction, making me more and more awake, even once Sadie and Isabel had stopped whispering.

I worried about the vase and what would happen when Isabel's parents realized it was missing. I worried about Isabel and how the thing I had done might get her in huge trouble. I worried about myself and how disappointed in me all of the grown-ups would be once they figured out the truth. I worried about Banana and whether she was wide awake, tossing and turning too, when she should be curled up sleeping.

I wished Maria hadn't given me that dare. I wished I hadn't said yes to it. I wished my balance had been better and that Mewsic hadn't run out in front of me and that I'd managed to catch the vase before it fell. I wished we'd never let Isabel's sisters play the game with us. I wished we hadn't had this sleepover at all.

I rolled over onto my left side, then my right side, then my back, but I couldn't get comfortable in any position. The floor felt hard beneath my body. My pillow felt too flat or too high or too lumpy, even though it was the same pillow that usually felt just right at home.

The house was eerily quiet, and I wished so much that I could hear Banana snoring softly in her basket next to my bed. I lay still, trying not to disturb Sadie and Isabel in their sleeping bags beside me, but the harder I tried not to move, the more fidgety I became. I watched the shadows and moonlight move across Isabel's walls in strange patterns, different from the ones I was used to at home. I'd spent so many hours playing in this room with my friends during daylight, but it felt really, really different late at night. It looked different; it sounded different; the air even tasted different. I loved my friends and usually my favorite place in the world to be was with them, but right now all I wanted was to be back at my own house, in my own bed, with my own dog sleeping beside me.

But I couldn't go home now. I was stuck.

"Sadie," I whispered, in case she was awake too. Sadie didn't move or answer.

I propped myself up on my elbow so I could see over her to Isabel. "Isabel," I said, a little louder. Isabel let out a light snore. She and Sadie were both sound asleep.

I thought about nudging Sadie awake or faking a coughing fit to wake up both of them, but I knew that wouldn't be fair. And what would I even say if I did wake them? That I missed my dog? That I felt bad about the vase? That I wanted to be back in my own bed? My friends couldn't fix any of that, even if they were awake. I let them keep sleeping. The night seemed endless.

I had never felt so alone.

Chapter Fifteen
Decisions, Decisions

I climbed out of my sleeping bag as quietly as I could and tiptoed into the hallway, where a night-light guided my way to the bathroom. I turned on the faucet, cupped my hands under the water, and drank a few sips. I dried my hands on a towel and opened the door to the medicine cabinet, not even sure what I was looking for. Inside, there was an extra tube of toothpaste, the same kind we used at my house. Seeing it made me feel both better and worse.

I shut the cabinet door.

I crept back into the hallway and noticed a

light on downstairs. Was somebody else awake? I wasn't sure if I might get in trouble for being out of bed, but I started down the stairs anyway. Maybe if one of Isabel's parents was still up, they would offer to drive me home to Banana.

Not that I wanted to leave my friends in the middle of the night, but I was feeling pretty homesick. Sadie and Isabel would probably understand.

I followed the glow of the light into the living room, where Abuelita was sitting in her armchair under a reading lamp, her feet up on a padded stool. Her glasses were perched halfway down her nose, and Mewsic was curled up on her lap. He was so gigantic that she couldn't fit both him and a paperback in her lap. She had to hold her book off to the side and prop it against the armrest instead.

Mewsic and Abuelita looked so content, I didn't want to disturb them. Seeing them reminded me of the hours I spent curled up on the sofa with Banana and a book—one of my favorite ways to read. When Banana and I were wrapped up in a story, we didn't like to be interrupted.

But when I started to leave the room, the floorboards creaked beneath my feet, and Abuelita looked up from her book. "Anna?" she said. I stopped. "Are you having trouble sleeping?" she guessed.

"Yes," I admitted. She tucked a bookmark into her book and closed it with one hand, stroking Mewsic's back with the other. I hesitated, then walked toward her.

I love Abuelita. I love that the first time we met her, she told Sadie and me we could call her Abuelita too, even though she isn't our real grandmother. She said she considers the best friends of her granddaughters to be her own "honorary grandkids." I'd asked her what "honorary" meant, and she'd said, "It means even though you're not my granddaughter, I am honored to treat you that way." She always makes me feel special and important like that.

I settled onto the arm of the couch, next to her chair. "Do you always stay up this late?" I asked.

"Not always," she said. "But sometimes when I get caught up in a really good book, I like to spend the quietest part of the day alone with it. Well, alone with it and Mewsic, of course." Mewsic blinked.

"I'm sorry to interrupt you," I said.

"No, no. I'd just reached the end of the chapter. It's good timing. Though now that Mewsic has settled in like this, I'm not sure he's going to want to let me up. Come, feel how hard he's purring."

I reached out a hand, and as I leaned closer,

I heard the steady motor of his purr. Abuelita nodded as I placed my hand on his back and touched his soft fur. Abuelita was right—he was purring so hard, his whole body was vibrating. I could feel his happiness right through my hand.

There was something calming and comforting about how pleased he was, and it almost made me want to laugh. I looked up at Abuelita, and we shared a smile.

In that moment I made a decision. "There's something I have to tell you," I blurted, before I could chicken out.

"Oh?" she asked.

I petted Mewsic again, for strength and good luck. "A bad thing happened, and it's kind of my fault."

Abuelita waited to hear more, but instead of

telling her, I turned and went to the cabinet where Emma had tucked away the evidence. I pulled out the bundle, brought it over to Abuelita, and unwrapped the broken vase.

Chapter Sixteen
Truth Be Told

Abuelita sucked in a surprised breath. "Oh. That is a bad thing," she said.

My insides felt like someone had chewed them all up and spit them back out again, like a used-up wad of gum. I was super worried what Abuelita might think of me now that she'd seen what I had done, but also, it was a relief having it out in the open. Even if I got into big, big trouble now, at least I wouldn't still be carrying a horrible secret.

"How did this happen?" she asked. Her voice sounded worried, not angry, but I still wasn't sure

 I should tell her the whole story. I wasn't breaking Isabel's promise by showing Abuelita the vase—Isabel had promised we wouldn't tell her parents, not that we wouldn't tell *anyone*—but still. It seemed better not to bring Truth or Dare and the sisters into it.

"I dropped it," I said. "I'm so sorry."

Abuelita nodded and stroked Mewsic's back. "Mistakes happen. But how did it end up wrapped in a tablecloth in the cabinet?"

I looked down at my feet. My pink sparkly toes didn't have any good answers. "I can't tell you without breaking a promise," I said.

Abuelita paused for a long moment. "I know how hard it can be to be honest when you've messed up and something's gone wrong. I'm glad you told me," she said. I looked up at her face. Her eyes were serious, but full of kindness. "And I know *you* know it's important to be careful with other people's things," she said. "Although it's even more important to be careful with their feelings."

"I know," I whispered. "I know the vase is special. I know that Isabel's parents will feel terrible because I broke it."

Abuelita reached out and took the bundle from me. She held it under the light to look. "Let me see. This might not be quite as bad as you think."

Hope fluttered inside me like a butterfly's wings. "It's not?"

Abuelita peered closely at the two broken halves

of the vase, then turned to me and smiled. "Did Isabel tell you the story of how her parents got this vase?"

"She said it's their wedding vase," I said.

"That's right. It was a gift to them from my mother, Isabel's great-grandmother." Abuelita handed the bundle back to me, and I set it carefully on the couch so the damage wouldn't get worse. She leaned back in her chair and scratched Mewsic under his chin. "But there's a little more to it than that. I'm not sure if Isabel even knows this part. You see, this vase carries a secret of its own."

Chapter Seventeen
The Secret History

I stared at Abuelita. What did that mean? "The vase has a secret?" I hadn't seen anything inside it.

She nodded. "Of sorts. You see, before the vase belonged to Isabel's parents, it belonged to her great-grandparents, Clara and Gio. Gio had given it to Clara on *their* wedding day, as a special gift for his bride."

I pictured Clara as an older version of Isabel, dressed in a fancy wedding gown from a hundred years ago, holding the brand-new vase. It made me sad to imagine her learning that I'd broken it.

"When Clara opened the gift from Gio and

saw the vase inside, she was surprised and delighted, but also concerned. You see, she had walked past the shop where these vases were made and admired their beauty in the window many times. But she knew the vases were incredibly expensive. They were handmade and painted by a very talented artist who sold them for a lot of money. Clara and Gio could not afford such a price."

Abuelita paused, and Mewsic nudged her hand to encourage her to keep scratching him and to continue telling the story. "So how did Gio get one, then?" I asked.

"That's what Clara wondered too," Abuelita

said. "She worried her new husband had spent all of their money—the money they needed for food and rent—on buying her the beautiful vase. She told him they would have to return it. But the gift could not be returned."

Mewsic and I both held perfectly still, waiting to hear what Abuelita would say next.

"You see, the vase was expensive, but Gio had not paid for it," she said.

"He *stole* it?" I asked. Even Mewsic looked shocked. But Abuelita shook her head.

"No, no. Gio was not a thief," she said. Mewsic and I exhaled in relief. "Gio told Clara the story of how he'd been standing outside the shop, admiring the vases in the window and dreaming of one day buying one for her. While he was doing this, a customer *inside* the store knocked one over, and the vase split in two."

"Oh no!" I said. I could imagine how horrible the customer must have felt.

"Yes, the vase was ruined," Abuelita said. "At least, the potter and the customer thought so. Gio watched from outside as they picked up the pieces. The customer paid for the damage, but he left the broken vase behind. What good was it to him now?"

I looked at the broken vase on the couch, then back at Abuelita. She nodded, even though I still didn't know where the story was going.

"Gio went inside and asked the potter what she would do with the broken pieces. 'Throw them away,' she said. 'The vase is ruined.' So Gio asked if he could have the two pieces for his bride."

"He glued the vase back together?" I guessed.

"That's right," Abuelita said. "It was no good to the potter, even fixed with glue, because it still had tiny cracks up the sides. It couldn't be sold as a vase because the cracks meant it couldn't hold water. But the vase was still beautiful, and it could still hold hope and the promise of a happy marriage—one that could

withstand a few cracks, falls, and fixes over time. Just like their friendship had. The vase became a symbol of Gio and Clara's promise that whatever happened in their lives together, whatever fights or disagreements they might have, they would always find a way to glue themselves back together."

I thought of the times Sadie, Isabel, and I had argued or even stopped speaking to one another and how finding ways to fix those problems had made our friendships even stronger. "So this vase has already been broken and then fixed," I said. "That's its secret."

"Yes. When you dropped it, it broke open along the same seam where it had already been broken before. And I bet we can glue it together again, just like Gio did the first time." Abuelita winked at me. "Should we try it? I think I have some glue in the kitchen."

Before I could answer, Mewsic leaped off her lap and headed for the kitchen door. We laughed.

I said, "I think that means yes."

Chapter Eighteen
Stuck Like Glue

We followed Mewsic to the kitchen, where Abuelita put a thin line of superglue along the broken edges of the vase and placed the two halves together. She instructed me on how to hold the pieces in place and apply just enough pressure (but not too much!)

to keep it steady while the glue set. Together, we counted slowly to a hundred while Mewsic wound between our legs and the glue started to dry. Then Abuelita nodded, and I let go.

The glue held! I knew there was still a crack in it, but the vase *seemed* just like new. You'd have to be looking carefully at the exact spot where the vase had broken to see it was damaged at all. I beamed at Abuelita. "Thank you," I said.

She hugged me. "You're welcome. Now, let's put this vase back on the shelf where it belongs, so the glue can dry completely while we sleep."

I yawned. Now that she mentioned it, I was feeling pretty sleepy.

Abuelita carried the vase to the living room and placed it on the bookshelf. "There. Now, off to bed. If you go quietly, no one will even know you were up. It's our secret."

I hugged her again, then tiptoed up the stairs and into Isabel's bedroom, where I slid back into my sleeping bag and cuddled Banana's bunny toy. I was certain now that Isabel was right: Banana had loaned me the toy on purpose, in case I needed it—which I had.

My sleeping bag and pillow felt much cozier now that I wasn't tossing and turning with a terrible secret. And even though I still missed having Banana there to sleep beside me, I knew I would see her soon. When I did, I would have a really good story to tell her.

I closed my eyes, and the next thing I knew, it was morning and my friends were shaking me awake.

Chapter Nineteen

Secrets Revealed

"Anna," Sadie said. "Wake up, sleepyhead. It's time to rise and shine."

I sat up and rubbed my eyes. Sadie and Isabel were already dressed. "You were out like a rock," Isabel said. "We thought you might have decided to sleep through the winter, like the hibernating skunks we learned about in science class."

"Hey!" I protested. "I'm not a skunk. I'd be a hibernating groundhog, maybe. Or a bat, so I could sleep upside down."

"Skunks are cute too," Isabel said. "*I'll* be the skunk if you don't want to be. Then I could spray my sisters with skunk juice to stop them from ruining our games."

I grinned at her. Isabel would make a silly skunk. But her face had gotten serious. "I think I have to break the promise," she said. "I've been thinking about it and thinking about it, and I need to tell my parents the truth about the vase. Even if it makes everyone mad at me, I have to tell them we broke it. Keeping it a secret just makes it even worse."

Sadie put her arm around Isabel's shoulders. "We'll help you tell them," she said. "Right, Anna?"

My new secret fizzed and sparkled inside me like soda. I couldn't wait for my friends to see that the vase had been fixed. "Absolutely," I said, and I meant it. But I had a feeling we'd be in a lot less trouble than she expected, thanks to Abuelita's late-night help. "Let's do it at breakfast," I suggested, knowing that before we did, I would find a way to show my friends the surprise.

Isabel took a deep breath and let it out with a whoosh. "Okay," she said.

I rolled up my sleeping bag, changed into my clothes, and tucked my pajamas and slippers and Banana's bunny into my backpack. When I turned back around, Sadie was holding three blank pieces of paper. "We forgot to read our secret wishes," she said.

The invisible ink! I'd forgotten all about it. "Want to do that now?" I asked.

"Yeah!" Isabel cheered. She seemed happy to delay the confession. "How do we do it again?"

"Heat makes the invisible ink turn visible, so we just have to warm up the pages with a hair dryer," Sadie said. She handed a paper to each of us. "I don't know whose is whose anymore, so we'll have to reveal them to find out."

We took the secrets into the bathroom, where Isabel got out the hair dryer from under the sink, plugged it in, and handed it to Sadie. Sadie turned it on low and started heating her paper. At first nothing happened. Then, slowly, parts of the paper started to turn brown where the lemon juice was.

"It's Mewsic! And Banana!" Sadie said. She was holding the wish I'd made.

Isabel peeked over her shoulder. "Aw, they're

adorable together.
I wish they could be
friends too." She grinned
at me. "Hey, we should make a comic about
their adventures together!" I smiled back. That
sounded like fun.

Sadie handed the hair dryer to Isabel, who
made the next secret wish appear. We watched as
the page went from blank to covered in a pattern
of hearts, stars, and swirls, like an explosion of
happiness.

"Did you draw that one?" Sadie asked. Isabel
nodded.

"It's so cool," I said. "What is it?"

"It's a wish for something exciting to happen,"
Isabel explained. Her shoulders drooped. "I
guess that one came true." She handed me the

hair dryer. "So, you must have Sadie's secret message," she said.

"Yup." I turned on the heat and held up the paper so we could see what it said: *Isabel + Sadie + Anna = Best Friends Forever.*

Isabel clapped and looked more cheerful again. "That secret wish will definitely come true."

Chapter Twenty

Purrfectly Okay

We returned our secret wishes to Isabel's room and tucked them inside her desk where no one would see them. "It's too bad the ink doesn't turn back to invisible once you've seen it," Isabel said.

Sadie shrugged. "You'd need a *really* magic lemon for that."

My stomach growled with hunger. "Did you hear that noise my belly made? It sounded like Mewsic's purring," I said.

Sadie giggled, but Isabel only nodded. "I guess we'd better feed it breakfast," she said.

Her words were cheerful, but her voice sounded nervous. Sadie and I looked at each other, then wrapped our arms around Isabel in a group hug.

"It's going to be okay," Sadie said. "However upset your parents might be, they will still be glad that you told them the truth. And Anna and I will do anything we can to help make things better. We'll help with extra chores and all of that."

"True," I said. "Whatever happens, we're in this together."

We dropped the hug and Isabel smiled, but I could tell she was still upset. I knew how awful she felt because I'd felt the same way last night. But I could help her feel better now, just like Abuelita had helped me. It was time to show her the secret.

"Hey, I have an idea. Before we eat and tell your parents, let's go find Mewsic," I said. "I bet petting him will help you feel stronger and more ready. It always helps me to hug Banana before I do something hard."

Isabel looked uncertain, but Sadie said, "Good idea."

"Maybe he's on the couch in the living room. Let's go check," I said. I took Isabel's hand and pulled her toward the staircase without giving her a chance to say yes or no.

We ran downstairs and into the living room, and I saw we were in luck: Mewsic was curled up on the couch, taking a catnap in a sunbeam. His eyes were half closed with happiness. Isabel stepped forward and cuddled herself around him. His whiskers twitched, and Isabel smiled as he started to purr. "Oh, Mewsic," she said.

At the same time Sadie said, "Oh my gosh!" She grabbed my arm. "Look!"

Sadie pointed toward the bookcase behind the couch, and Isabel sat up to see what Sadie was staring at. When she saw the vase, unbroken and sitting where it belonged, she shrieked. Mewsic bolted off the couch. I laughed.

"Is that . . . is it . . . is it real?" Isabel stammered.

Sadie turned toward me, her mouth still hanging wide open. I bounced on my heels with delight.

Isabel's eyebrows were the highest I'd ever seen them. "Do you know anything about this?" she asked.

I couldn't help but smile. "Maybe," I said. "Really the person you should ask is Abuelita."

Isabel's mom appeared in the doorway. "Good morning. Everybody sleep okay?"

Isabel and Sadie were still too shocked to respond, so I answered for all of us. "Yup!" I said.

"Great. What are you all up to in here?" she asked.

"Oh. We were just, um, talking about that vase," I said, motioning toward it. "I—"

Before I could say more, Maria cried, "Wait!"

and rushed in from the other room. "The vase," she said, panting, "it's my fault. I'm the one who dared her. I'm so sorry." Isabel's mother's eyes went wide with surprise. She had no idea what Maria was talking about, of course.

Emma appeared in the doorway behind Maria. "It's my fault too," she blurted. She turned to Isabel and me. "We discussed it last night and decided we can't let you—" Her words ended with a squeak when she saw the repaired vase behind us. "It's—how did it—how did you—I mean . . ." she said, stepping toward it. Maria saw it too, and gasped.

"My goodness," Isabel's mother said. "What has gotten into all of you this morning?"

Maria blinked several times, like she still couldn't believe what she was seeing. Abuelita stuck her head into the room, caught my eye, and winked. "You know, that vase has a very special story that goes with it. Come on into the kitchen for breakfast, and I'll tell you all about it," she said.

She left, and Maria, Emma, and Isabel's mother followed after her, all looking confused.

My friends stared at me. I grinned at them. "This secret's too good not to share."

Acknowledgments

Much of this story was drafted by hand at Rosedale Dog Park and Nomad Pizza. Thanks to all of the very good dogs who chased and played with my pup, Arugula, while I wrote, and to the staff at Nomad in Princeton for the delicious salad, pizza, and ice cream that sustained me. Thank you, Princeton Public Library, for providing a quiet place to type and revise, and for all the great books you've loaned me.

Hugs to everyone at the Stonington Public Library in Stonington, Maine, especially Jill Anderson Larrabee and Vicki Zelnick, for inviting me back home for special events with cupcakes, craft projects, and kid readers. Special thanks to my friends in the Deer Isle-Stonington community who have been so supportive of my writing endeavors. I was lucky to grow up in a place full of good storytellers and interesting characters.

Thanks to the students, librarians, and educators

who have welcomed Anna, Banana, and me into their schools and classrooms, in person and via Skype. Talking with kids about books and writing is one of my favorite parts of being an author. Thanks to An Open Book Foundation for connecting authors with readers and giving us the chance to create new stories together.

Truth: This sleepover would be only half as fun without the smart suggestions and sparkly polish provided by my editor, Alexa Pastor. Thanks to everyone at S&S who helps with the series, including Laurent Linn, Audrey Gibbons, Katrina Groover, Martha Hanson, Justin Chanda, Anne Zafian, and Kristin Ostby. Thank you, Meredith Kaffel Simonoff, for being the hair dryer to my lemon juice. Cassey Kuo: Welcome to the party!

Thank you to the friends and family who dare me to take creative risks and support me through every triumph and setback. Extra love to Grammy, who reads every book, and to Mama and Ati, who have not-so-secretly been my champions from the start.

Collect all seven books in the Anna, Banana series!

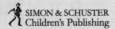

JOIN THIRD-GRADE SCIENTIST AND INVENTOR EXTRAORDINAIRE ADA LACE AS SHE SOLVES MYSTERIES USING SCIENCE AND TECHNOLOGY!

One school musical . . .

Two third graders destined for stardom . . .

And a lead role that goes to the wrong girl!

A new chapter book series from young
Academy Award–nominated actress Quvenzhané Wallis.